Daisies & daffodils

Dedications:

To my Mother,
Who stood by me through it all.
To my Father,
Who never let me doubt my place in life.
To the loves of my life,
Who allowed me to find these words.
To myself, for everything.

From the stem of all problems,
Falling petals of my heart.
I am rising from the dirt of my past,
I am blossoming into yours truly,
-Daisies and Daffodils

Secret Language

These fonts were seen from the stories before,
Each one with a tale that only I am sure.
Previous pages you have flipped,
recent words your eyes sipped.
These scripts speak louder than my voice could carry,
You may continue but those included be wary.
I do not shy from telling my truth,
So listen to the fonts,
before you continue on your sleuth.

A broken mind in a dying body,

A crippling soul best described as beauty.

She was trembling, yet appeared as though laughing,

After all when you stare at a mosaic you never see

shattered pieces, you see art.

"I'm the happy one..."
 I whisper as a stream of tears
cascade down my rosy cheeks.
"I'm the happy one..."
I cry as I look in the eyes of someone
who needs me far more then I need them.
"I'm the happy one..."
I scream in a pitch only I can hear,
as I sit in a room full of people
who never seem to realize
"I'm the happy one"
..but I'm not happy

Hair like honey.
Freckles like stars.
The Delirious lust drips runny,
But dries thick like tar.

Time and time again,

I search for forever in momentarily people.

A lesson never learned,

an experience never taught.

I fall again each time from higher lengths,

Hoping this time,

This time he will catch me.

Perhaps my luck has run out or my jumps not

centered, for every time I fall, I miss.

Blond strands that shift of golden delight,
A consistent mind traffic I can not fight.
His voice as smooth as a liquor shot,
So engulfed by him, goodbye I can not.
He is a trapping and aching pool of tar,
Yet it fears me more to be afar.

It is the ones you never expect to fall in
love with that hurt the most.
Like jumping off a bench and suddenly
the ground that seemed so close
moments before, vanishes without any
sense of security or guidance.
It is like falling into the dark,
When will you let me hit the ground?

It is growing harder to
separate you from the others.
The more I look to them,
I want to see you.
The more I look at you,
the less I want to see them.

Like bubbles brewing upon their
waters creeping to escape.
It is a build up, a desire,
a strive for a feeling,
I keep edging to feel you,
let me boil over.

The grumbles taste like skinny,
The food tastes like fat.
"I can keep going" she cries
As her life line goes flat.

So many hot tears pooled up and scurried down my cheeks at the thought of losing you again, I let them fall.
So many words I wish I could scream to you and let you know just how much you hurt me again, I let them out.
So many thoughts ran rapid through my head trying to tie together every word you said over again, I let them circulate.
So many realizations shooting back once I remember who I became without you in my life again, I let them process.
So little worry, fueled my emotions when I realized I was going to be okay without you again, I let you go.

You Held the handle, I held the blade.
Maybe I hung onto long,
Maybe I squeezed too hard,
Maybe I loved too much,
You held the handle, I held the blade.
My hand grew tired,
My skin cut deep,
My heart ached Louder, You held the
handle, I held the Blade.
You lost your grip,
You let us go,
You let go of the handle...
I died holding the blade.

I read the words I used to write,
where all the happy was out of sight.
I long to write with that much heart,
I long but still I can not start.
My minds not dreary with ache and pain,
My heads not fogged with clouds or rain.
This emotion is foreign, scary and new,
This emotion is stirring all thanks to you.
The weary tales grow dusty on the rack,
For As of now, you brought my happy back.

I remember the first day we met,
The sun danced circles on your hair
in hues only I could see.
I remember the first day we met,
My eyes covered you like a blanket on a
cold day, yet you never felt the touch.
I remember the first day we met,
No words exchanged just glances of
strangers, two crossing paths who would
not overlap until later.
I remember the first day we met,
Even if you never do.

You were not the one,
a part of me always knew that.
But, for a brief moment,
you made me never wanna find them.

It's getting bad again,
No one seems to know,
No one seems to care.
It's getting bad again,
The tears are coming back,
The pain is seeping through.
It's getting bad again,
I don't know who I am,
I don't know what to do.

Our blood once ran hot, scolding as fire.

It now runs cold, Freezing like ice.

The soothing blanket of cool, masked my mind.

Covered the memories I wanted to forget

Funny thing with these elements,

I always seem to forget,

both sides hurt.

Both sides burn.

wish to watch you cross oceans.
One, because I wish to see you succeed,
Two, because I just like watching you.

I stare at doors as if you will walk through them,
As If you would realize you were wrong.
As if it dawned on you I was the one all along,
That I was the ending you were supposed to get.
The life we were destined to live resided in us
being together.
As if you realized you messed up.
But every time someone else walks through.
You never realize it,
You never feel guilty,
Or muster up a way to apologize.
You never regret it.
I am starting to think you never will.

He has my favorite heart,
As If he took the good in me, and kept it.
It is not that I miss him,
I miss me.

I keep searching for someone else,
Yet I can not figure out if it is because I want to
move on, or make you jealous.
I think deep down I know that I can not succeed
because I am looking for you in everyone I find.
Even worse, I know that there is no one out there
like you.

A letter to my first love,

It's been a while, I hope you are well. Although you haven't been here watching my life like a movie I feel like a part of you will still show up in the ending credits. I think a part of you will always be with me. It's the love I had for you that taught me what I wanted next. I've been hurt a lot since you were here. I've loved and hated and loved all over again. I've been smitten, head over heels and heartbroken all in one swoop. They say you never get over your first love and I suppose it's true, not in the way i had originally expected though. I don't get that heat of jealousy when I see you with her, I get a different kind of warmth, one that encapsulates my heart with the knowledge you got everything you wanted, everything you deserved. I don't stay up thinking of our future, I think of my own. But every once in a while when you flutter in my mind I think of yours too, similar to parallel lines running next to each other, Moving in the same direction but never overlapping. I often think of how lucky I am to know you as my first love, how lucky I was to feel so much for someone so special. So yes I suppose they are right, that amongst all my loves you are the one I can't seem to forget, but how lucky am I to have someone I don't wish to forget. I will always have a small part of my heart set aside to you, it's just now it's in a different spot, shining in a different way. as years go by, as more life forms around us I no longer feel riddled with sadness you aren't here with me but rather overjoyed I get to watch you from afar. You have a beautiful soul and I'm so lucky that even for a moment I got to be in its presence. Thank you for the lessons, the wisdom but most importantly,
thank you for the love, it was my first.

I make up stories of you to help me sleep,
Little plays being acted out by versions
of us that do not exist.
I find peace in having you love me,
even if it is fictional.
As If I take any shred of you,
instead of losing you completely.
I often wonder if I have gone crazy,
if I have truly lost my mind.
But it is when I start to drift asleep
and the worries fade...
I remember it is not an absence of sanity,
It is simply just the absence of you.
You always did know how to make my heart and
mind go different directions.

What happens when you pour water
from separate taps in the same cup?
One tainted by chemicals and past,
The other clear and pure.
Does the cup grow merky does it ruin
the clarity?
Or does it defog the ruins of the other?
Equal parts,
Too extreme to ever collide.

I swear my love for you crossed oceans
For even if there was no eyes to see it
my wave of love roared large.
My love for you felt storms and calm
waters, felt clear skies and howling wind.
My love for you built up so high when my
final stretch of passion curled over,
I found myself on shore.
Maybe parts of my love crawled back into
the habits of the past like the tide of the
beach, but most of it lingered on the
sand.Parts of me will always be with you
but the rest is finally still.

I am crippled by the fear that one day I will be sitting in the life always dreamed, and you will not be there. Then suddenly, the dreams I held so close were not the ones I wanted to be chasing.

Loving you,
Fucking blows.

Skipping stones,
find, release, watch
It is poetic is it not?
The beauty in selecting something just to set
it free,
As if it was only yours for a moment,
or if it really was yours at all.
Skipping stones,
find, release, watch
If only it were that easy,
To know which things were going to work
out
and which would sink.
Skipping stones,
find, release, watch
Because at the end of it all,
even when you choose right
and you let it go that can not be it,
You watch, watch them succeed watch
them sink.
Just to show up on shore and let someone
else try.
Skipping stones,
find, release, watch
That is all we are now,
found, released and watching.

I am the girl you meet along the way,
The one that walks you towards the one you say
yes to.
I am the one who patches you up,
just enough to keep you together.
I work on the things people abandon you for,
I am the girl you like a lot but never really love.
I am the girl you meet along the way,
The one who brings your smile back.
I am the one who checks in
and pushes you to be better,
I help even when you don not want me to.
I am the girl you want today but not tomorrow.
I am the girl you meet along the way,
The one who tells you everything
is going to be alright.
I am the one whose heart breaks
when you find the one.
I wish you well even when I do not want to,
I am the girl who watches the vows from the
back of the church.
I am the girl you meet along the way,
The one who loved you enough
to be just a pit stop.

I am not sad about losing you,
I am sad about losing the version of myself
that only exists in your presence.
I am okay with you not wanting me anymore,
but I need her, in order to want myself.

Maybe one day we will find closure in the
emotions we once felt.
I will be able to poke fun
at the desire I felt for you.
And you, perhaps you could open up to
the thoughts that once plagued your mind.
Maybe one day,
we can appreciate what it was,
rather than what we wanted it to be.

I Love you.

I wish I got to tell you that.

It would appear I am too
No, not the number in which describes my age,
Nor the middle word used to explain a distance
between other things.
I am too.
I am too talkative, even when spoken to.
I am too loud, even when encouraged to speak up.
I am too big for the fantasy of beauty.
I am too annoying for the dream of love.
I am too scared in a world that has only
given me reason to be.
I am too stupid to compare thoughts with others.
I am too excited even if it is something to be so.
I am too female to hold my own.
I am too much.
In a world as grand as this, how is it possible
I am too much?
In a world as wide spread and limitless how can
I be too much?
In a world so driven in telling us we are not enough…
how could someone simply be TOO?

It would appear I am too.

No, not the number in which describes my age,

Nor the middle word used to explain a distance

between other things.

I am too.

Too smart to allow foolish opinions cloud my own.

Too confident to even fathom others thoughts being

more powerful then my own.

Too sure that I am exactly who I am supposed to be.

I may be too,

but not too much,

too good.

Sometimes I think you are the only one
who ever really met me.
As If I were a stranger to the familiar souls in my life.
A momentary flame in an orchestra of fire,
you saw me.
It is terrifying to stare at the devil
and only seen proximity.
So even if you were not the only one who saw me,
I suppose you were the only one I wanted to.

For years,
I wished you had glances at me the way you
longed for them,
For you to see past my excess figure.

For years,
I wanted to be the only thing you
thought about,
For you to see how much I cared.

For years,
 I watched from afar,
For you to never notice.

" When he picks on you he likes you "
So, when her 5th grade crush pushed
her off the swing,
she thought he liked her.
When her 9th grade boyfriend sent that photo around
of her, because he wanted to " show her off "
she thought he liked her
When her 11th grade boyfriend pleaded
" you didn't say no "
she thought he liked her.
When her fiancé left those bruises on her arms
she swore were from a " biking accident "
she thought he liked her
When she laid limp on the bathroom floor losing
vision,
she thought he, Loved her.

It is the decisions that you least expect to make, that help you the most.

Life in a Fishbowl

I have lived my life in a fishbowl,
Exposed and vulnerable to anyone who had the time to
look.
I am an open book, a crystal clear window, an empty
glass box.
I am as free to you as an ant among a meadow.
I have lived life in a fishbowl,
Trapped and insecure with the fear of all eyes on me,
I am shaken soul, a quivering body, an embarrassment
of sight.
I am as scared of you as prey to its predator.
I have lived my life in a fishbowl,
Filled with hatred and guilt for the people who shadow
my sunshine.
They are my biggest enemies, my strongest fears, my
saddest of tales.
I have lived my life in a fishbowl,
With an ignorance to the fact even with the hate I have
to the world around me,
I would die without it.

A single crack shakes through a drought ridden desert,
across the world a stream of water rushes through a
luscious forest.
The dryness takes over its own self, swallowing any
moisture surrounding it.
The stream runs powerful breaking any barrier
holding it back,
Both traveling fast,
Never to touch.
Until a brisk April morning washed over the sky,
And the powerful stream gracefully danced between
the crack of the desert.
Not soon after the water dried up,
It swallowed me,
And I let it.

Beststranger

Stranger, stranger I used to know,
Tell me where, oh where you go.

Are you hiding from me in fear of truth?
Or roaming the lust that comes with youth.

You called me friend not long ago,
Now dear old friend your care is low.

I miss our days of laughs and jokes,
Before your love was clouds of smokes.

Stranger stranger I used to know,
My sight of you is growing low.

You are not who I once did know,
My memory of you is dying slow.

Our friendship now is oh so slim,
Stay true to your choice, your choice of him.

Little by little,
The air grew a little thicker,
My knees a little weaker,
My breath a little shorter,
And my heart a little faster,
And that is when I knew,
Little by little,
I was falling in love with you.

A single rain drop fell upon my skin today,
The shivering touch trickled down my chest,
I squirmed to take the pain away,
It was just as cold as you were.

When I think of you and I
And The love that made us tie,
I think of all the love I gave
And all the love you did not save,
I think of how your love ran out
As you walked out the door without a shout,
My love I hope this next one is right
This one that is the lady of night,
When I think of you and I
And the love that made us tie,
I ponder for a moment and shed a small tear
Till I remember you were never really here.

Carved out like a statue
standing tall in a museum.
Chiseled with the utmost
attention to detail,
You are perfect.
A soul so pure it could bring light
back to an entire room.
So closed off only few can see it,
You are perfect.
Both physical, emotionally and spiritually
You are perfect.
I just wish you could see it.

Love is
Hopeless and fear,
Reliabilities,
A terrifying test of truth,
Love is.

Parts of me sometimes show,
Old versions of me, would never know,
Every tear, every scream,
May never leave this writing scheme.

I have seen many people walk past me
and stared,
I am beauty, I am hatred, I boost and
I'm scared.
My truth causes pain, and my lies
make me broken,
I am sorry my gift was a self hatred
token.
They are not ugly, not bad and yet they
still fear,
The opinion they hear when they look
in my mirror.

She was a friend until today

I did not mean to hurt her,
I did not intend to do the damage.
She was my world,
My person,
My true best friend.
I did not purposely throw it all out the window,
I did not focus on the pain I had caused.
She was my rock,
My home,
My sunshine in rain,
I did not know what I had done till it was far too late,
I did not know I would feel like this without her here,
She was a friend until today.

My hinges grew rusty with each year that had passed,
My door knob more brassy each year that it lasted.

I made it to triple digits with dust bunnies to spare,
I made it here with lots of musk in the air.

I had not been opened since the old owners left me,
I had not seen light rays since the torch flame got flaky.

If only the world could see past my door of old,
If only they knew I was where they hid the gold.

I fear as though my love bleeds thick,
Poured out like syrup and coughs like sick.

It is encased within a thinning vein,
Wishing to fall right out as if it is rain.

My fears grow more and more they do,
It's terrifying to know,
I am in love with you.

The moon,
An odd comfort, it is.
When you know it is lingering
in the clouds waiting for light.
When it rises from the horizon,
showing you it has been there all day.
Maybe we always know it is there,
Maybe we just choose to think
it is only there on the endless nights,
or when the sky is full of its shape.
Maybe, we only want to believe that it is
there sometimes because the thought of it
always being there,
well that means somethings really do
never change.

I did not want this,
I did not want these words in my head.
But I got it, much to my dismay,
this is what I was dealt,
I made a hell of a lot with it.
That is not gratitude that is acceptance.

I worry for the way you lend your heart out
As if a trial for people to use and break.
I fear you will never give it to one who will
truly care for it the way they should,
Never love you like you deserve.
I suppose It is my own fault,
that I mind it the way I do.
Deep down I know the reason I worry so
much for your heart is because I now how
much I wish it were me you gave it to.

How sad temptation feels when taunted with
something you could never have.
An emotion that cannot be fulfilled,
an itch that cannot be scratched.

So tell me why when the world is falling around
me the only voice I want to hear is yours,
a voice I have heard whispered for years and
looked past, now suddenly shouting in my ear.

I found you covered in water,
On a beach where everything seemed
shinier when wet.
I picked you in the dozen,
as if you wanted me to,
as if it was planned.
How beautiful you would be encased on display.
Though the water started to dry,
the beauty began to fade,
and then just like that,
you were like any rock on the beach,
nice to look at,
not to keep.

A ferociously palpitating heart
Encased in a rusted cage.
Trapped, strained, agony,
Each time it attempts to flee the acid lined
barriers burn into its core.
For it can never leave, not without feeling all
the pain it is meant to first.

I always said I wanted to live life like a movie,
as though my biggest dreams and strongest desires
would all fall perfectly into the template
of a story already written.
Though, the time line went haywire
and the plot began to slip and suddenly I realized,
perhaps my favorite stories were that because of
their lack of reality.
The absence of human factuality,
yanked them away from being obtainable.

I never thought I could linger
on ones basic functions,
until I fell in love with the
rise and fall of your chest.
As you lay behind my arm
that rests so comfortably upon you,
I realize the breaths you take
have become my favorite thing to notice.
Perhaps it is the reminder you are there,
or the comfort that you are not
a figment of my imagination.

I do not want your name to be on my tongue,
Your voice to be in my head,
Your face in my memories,
I do not want our past to clog my future,
I do not want to write about you anymore,
I do not want to love you anymore.

I often forget how quickly the fog takes over,
how one minute you sense the moisture,
and the next you are engulfed in it.
I often forget how lonely being the sunshine is,
being the one whose sole purpose
was to help the fog dance away from others.
I often stop and breathe in the fog I am apart of
and wonder if by pulling it from others,
did I burden it on myself?
I often wonder why I see the fog so thick around others,
as though they are pleading for help out
and yet no one sees mine.
I often hope it is because my sunshine
blinds them from the truth.
I often tell myself that, even when I know it is a lie.
I often believe it,
not because I should, but because I want to.

When the sun blankets over the life
you never thought you would live,
your eyes let in a little more colour,
your heart grows a little bit bigger,
and your soul feels a little bit fuller.
It is a beautiful thing to dream,
it is even better to stick around to see them come true.

That lump in my throat burns again,
The same feeling from when it all began.
The empty chest and hollow heart,
Begins to reminisce from the start.
I am scared of this, terrified it is true,
But I am used to it now, it is nothing new.
My pain runs deep like the etches in rocks,
I fear it will last longer than allowed on clocks.

And maybe it was the speckles on your face
that seemed to only look richer in the sun

Or the way the fabric of your shirt cascaded
softly over your chest, but tightly on your
arms

Maybe it was the flutter of your eyelashes
when you looked away and back

Or the laugh in your throat that had
movement like thunder but volume like wind

I do not know what made me look at you
differently that day, maybe I never will

Or maybe I already do.

I do not wish to know the pain
of people who fear to say it,
But more the people who never get to know it.
For love, in its beauty and enchantment,
is also one of fear and anguish.

StockHOME

Small towns are a funny thing,
A place where solitude takes new meaning,
And freedom feels limits.
As I drive on the roads I once took to sleepovers,
or corners turned while crying after a fight.
I realize this solitude,
this cage feels smaller than when I left,
Its limits feel tighter, its sun seems duller.
Perhaps I have adapted to a larger tank,
or simply found more beauty far away.
Yet somehow every once and a while,
I feel home yank me back,
like an under-toe I can not out swim.
I fear I am drowning and I do not know whats worse,
Letting it consume me,
Or die trying to fight it.

And I know I love you
by the way I watch you love her,
because even though it is not me.
You are happy, and deep down
that is all I ever wanted.

Perspective is a wondrous thing when you start to realize the power it wields,

When you start to notice the mountains only show half the time, and city lights often go unnoticed.

When the puddle you stepped in soaks up and later falls on a drought.

Or when you trip on a branch that fell mere moments ago but has been growing for over a century.

When a cool chill of wind sneaks up your spine as it slowly fades from its hurricane.

Or perhaps a persons laugh dances in your ear so effortlessly all while it has been suppressed for weeks.

Perspective is a wondrous thing when you start to realize how much it means, and how little you have.

My greatest fears do not dangle from webs,
or views from high altitudes.

My fears do not rumble in the clouds,
or lurk as creatures in the night.

My greatest fears are not written into children books,
or used to fuel campfire stories.

My truest fear is the possibility I will never feel
the desire all my comfort literature characters do,
I will never have him watch as the sun hits
my eyes just right, or my laugh send shivers down his
spine, my fear is one that paralyzes, because in a world
where love is everything.. I fear I may never find it.

Sometimes, I wake up in fear at the thought of you leaving me, then I remember you were never mine to lose.

I wonder if you remember the drive,
If you felt that feeling of being alive.

I ponder if you miss the past,
for me that feeling was my last.

I fear to me it was far more than to you,
if you shudder when you remember it too.

Perhaps it was just a summer romance,
But I sure do wish it was given a chance.

For I do not know if I ever see anyone true,
quite like the way I once saw you.

Skipping rocks

1,2,3 each tapping ever so slightly
yet letting an infinity of ripples escape.

You made me feel like a skipping rock,
each pulse of my heart sent shudders of
memories through my soul.

I do not know how many pulses you made or
how many shudders are still there.

But I sure do hope you were happy with your
throw.

I hate to break the news to the ones
longing for a place in my books,
the people who desire a dedication in these pages.

The people whose essence are printed in this ink
are not ones I wish to glorify.

These souls, these stories, are not hero's or guides, they
are paths I have taken along a journey of survival.

Please do not be sad you are not here, I do not want you
to be.

I often wish I never allowed this door to be open,
this view into my mind be seen.

I do not want people to find out which font they are
hidden behind, yet I itch for them to read.

I long for the moment someone resonates with my
words, so why do I fear the thought of eyes on them?

In a way I think we all love the thought of success...
but only when it is on the brink of failure.

Confidence.

Such a funny word, it is.

Such a enchanting and longing word

Such a desire and craving

Such a jealousy driven persona

Such a inspiring and beautiful state

Such a lie and deception

Such a work in progress

Confidence.

It is a never ending battle

It is a two sided knife

It is a plot hole

It is a sham

It is the most precious belonging

It is a hoax

But even after all of this, it is all we really want, deep down we know it is the only thing we need.

Confidence.

An elaborate game of fake it till you make it.

The Ignorance of Privilege

I'm not privileged.
I say as my ivory skin soaks up the sun
on the beach that once hung a sign that screamed
"whites only"

I'm not privileged.
I whine as my blue eyes carry me through my job interview
I wouldn't have gotten if we didn't "have connections"

I'm not privileged.
I scream as new people join me on my side of the street
because the locals look
"intimidating"

I'm not privileged.
I think to myself eating dinner I
"expected" when I got home
I'm not privileged.

I'm oblivious.

Tides change quickly,
one moment we are staring at an endless ocean,
The next the truth peels back and it is nothing
more then dirt riddled sand.
Once a ferocious force of nature,
now a ridged cracked landscape.

Do you remember that hug?
The one in the driveway?
A goodbye I never wanted to give.
I often wonder what you were thinking
at that moment.
I often wonder if you felt what I felt.
Most of my memories of you are left with gaps,
gaps of never really knowing how you felt.
So, do you remember that hug?
Because I do.
Everyday I remember it.
Everyday I wonder if you do to.

As people we like to find similarities in others,
We search to find ourselves in other people.
Maybe it is to make us not feel crazy,
or perhaps just less alone.
We want to know that deep down someone
hurts just like us,
They feel just like we do.
At the end of it all,
the only thing we share with others
is that we are all alone.
Even together,
We are all just painfully and miserably alone.

I had assumed the worst was already done,
That the hurt had surpassed its limits.
But as I stare at that message,
I stare at the years of history it erases.
A hot tear trickles down my cheek like it is
scorching a path behind it.
You knew all the things I hated myself for,
and that is exactly how you left me.

" You're making my life more complicated than it needs to be "

My eyes read the message,
it is physically there and yet it is not.
Because you would not have said that,
you know my doubt too strong,
You know I would not move on from that.

As though our souls are tied in toxins,
My Effortless love,
Your inability to care for another.

One day he will long for me,
in all the ways I begged you to glance.
He will talk to me,
when all I asked was for your whisper.
He will hold me close,
where I settled for your brush in passing.
He will love me the way I deserve,
The way you did not.
The way you never will.

There is not much stronger than hate,
For only one thing I know that seals that fate.
A burning desire with no care for pain,
One emotion so powerful in its strain.
I felt it once, I think I did,
With fear and worry I kept it hid.
Perhaps one day he will know it well,
I fear for now I can not tell.
For if he leaves me high and dry,
I fear this feeling will simply die.
So I hold it close, so no one knows,
I keep it with me wherever I goes.
Heaven help me, oh lords above,
With him it is all I know, with him it is love.

Happily following you blind,
Religious loyalty

Two Toned

Stuck between two versions of myself,
As if I am mourning the girl I left behind,
And scared to meet the girl she is becoming.
A world of what ifs, and should I's
So toxically obsessed with the things I don not know.

I hold onto the fact we could come back,
That the stars will align just for us.
Rivers will run in hopes for us to witness them.
I hold onto the fact that maybe,
if I wish hard enough,
you will love me even half of how I loved you

Your name seems to be everywhere,
I can not figure out if it is because it is common
or because I am looking for it.

Honestly, I miss your mom.
I hope she is doing okay.

Someone told me you were not
kind to her,
For a moment,
even briefly I felt bad.
I felt bad that she does not know
the version of you I did.
I felt bad about that,
not about you, or her.

Would you believe me
if I told you I would not forgive you?
That I could not move on from the things
you said? the hurt you caused?
Would you believe that I have moved on?
Ya... me either.

Terrified you have moved on,
Terrified I never will.

You ruined my favorite movies,
You ruined my favorite songs,
You ruined my favorite weather,
You ruined everything,
You ruined me.

How lucky you are
to have been loved by me

Shivering shakes with echoing cries,
Repeating screeching versions of your lies,
My last remaining will slowly dies.

When the rain falls just right,
on the sill of your window after a cloudy day...
I hope you think of me.
When that song plays over the radio or in a store, and
your brain takes you back,
I hope you think of me.
When you pass by the row of orange juice at the grocery
store in our hometown,
I hope you think of me.
When someone mentions Nicolas sparks,
I hope you think of me.
When you hear The Lumineers,
I hope you think of me.
When you see someone singing in the car,
I hope you think of me.
When you play that stupid board game
that I only played to be competitive,
I hope you think about me.
When you go on each day living life,
I hope you think about me.
And when all you ever do is think of me,
when it is the only thought that clouds your mind,
maybe then you will understand why I was so upset,
because every time you think about me, I am already
thinking about you.
And it hurts.

There is this silly little thing I do where I
write down all the things you said to me that
I do not want to forget.
As If by having them there I can hold onto
you a little bit longer.
I think it boils down to my fear of it not
being real, but there is proof so it has to be.
I believe in my heart that if I never forget the
things you said, I will never forget how I felt.
They are some of my most and least
favorite memories, all mixed together into a
terrifying box of emotions.
I do not look at it often,
only when I really need to feel.

I miss you,
and I hate you for that.

3218 km away,
a world apart.
I would have traveled that.
Hell I would have moved right back
if you had asked.
It is funny how even though I know it is
the last thing I want to do.
I would do it for you.

Funny how the only time things are
real is once they are over,
only ever written in stone when they
have trickled into the past.
I had survived 18 when I turned 19,
I survived you once you finally left.

"You are probably better off without me"

That was not your choice.
It was not your call.
You do not get to decide
who I am around
and who I am not.

Between constant rise and fall of sleep
It was as though you were back to me.
My mind short circuiting different scenes
You were back and I was not alone.
And when the unfortunate blanket of reality
lays heavily atop my mind I realize,
In a fraction of a second I went from having
you right there to being alone again.
It is amazing how much it hurt,
as if it was actually happening.

I believe myself to be the luckiest person in the world
Not for having the prefect fleet of numbers on the lottery,
Or the broadcast name of the contest winner.
My luck runs deeper, my luck runs pure.
When I look at my luck,
I see tired checks from hours of laughing.
I see careless freedom in a lack of judgment.
My luck talks about anything and everything,
It is seen, heard and experienced,
my luck is a furthering of my own self.
My luck is my people,
yet my people make me the luckiest of them all.

Bittersweet endings were always my favorite, when you cant wait for the finale but dread the home stretch.

This isn't goodbye forever, thats why this visit was so short.

This story isn't finished, its only just begun.

I have some life to live and some stories to experience, maybe even some heartbreak to feel, or love to feel butterflies over before I can tell you all about it.

Its spring time and I suppose its my time to bloom. I'll miss you dear readers, but until next time look for me in the flowers, see you soon.

-Daisies & Daffodils

Daisies & daffodils

About The Author

"Daisies & Daffodils" is Maggie Grace's second collection of poetry. Following her Poetry debut with "Lemongrass" in 2019, she has expanded her poetry to following the life of a young adult navigating in a time unlike any other. Grace speaks on the emotional tolls embedded in her generation alongside the exposure of technology and social media. Open these pages, and be egullfed in the world of young love, body image and mental health.

Printed in Great Britain
by Amazon

24405076R00126